The Trouble With Buster

by Janet Lorimer
Illustrated by Emily Arnold McCully
Cover illustration by Carol Newsom

A
LITTLE APPLE
PAPERBACK

SCHOLASTIC INC.
New York   Toronto   London   Auckland   Sydney

ISBN 0-590-42641-9

Text copyright © 1990 by Janet Lorimer.

Illustrations copyright © 1990 by Scholastic Inc.

12 11 10 9 8 7 6 5 4 3 2 1   0 1 2 3 4 5/9
Printed in the U.S.A.   28

First Scholastic printing, January 1990

*For my dear friends, Chan and Nancy Rowe,
who finally convinced me
that my writing life was incomplete
without a word processor, guided my selection,
and then helped me tame the Beast.
With love and gratitude.*

CHAPTER 1

The trouble with Buster began the week my little sister, Bernice, started first grade. My sister is a big pain. She always wants to tag along, everywhere I go. She wants to play with all my stuff, even though she's got her own toys. And she's a tattletale. "Mom, Danny's getting a cookie. Can I have a cookie, too?"

That's when Mom comes storming into the kitchen. "What's wrong with you, Danny? You know we're going to have dinner in less than an hour. Do you want to spoil your appetite?" (It depends on what we're having for dinner. If it's liver or cauliflower . . . . But I don't tell Mom that.)

Like I said, kid sisters are a real pain, but

the big trouble began when Bernice started school.

In one way, I was looking forward to having Bernice go into the first grade, because I figured she'd learn to do a bunch of things on her own and quit bugging me to read to her and push her on the swings and stuff like that. She'd make new friends, too. On the other hand, I wasn't looking forward to Bernice walking to school and back home each day with me and my best friend, Rick.

"Come on, Mom," I begged. "It's not fair. Bernice is such a baby. Rick's going to be mad if we have to have Bernice tagging along with us every day."

"I am not a baby," Bernice yelled.

"See? See? She's such a whiner."

Mom glared at both of us. "Danny, stop calling your sister names. Bernice, stop yelling. I'm going to take Bernice to school the first morning, Danny, but after that you will walk her to and from school. She's just too little to walk by herself."

"I'm not little," Bernice yelled. "You all

treat me like I'm a baby. But I'm not."

Mom smiled and patted Bernice on the head. "I know, sweetheart," she said. "You're Mommy's big girl, and you're going to start school. And won't that be fun?"

Yuck! I wanted to throw up. Even Bernice was mad.

The first day of school Bernice was happy and scared all at the same time. She had a new dress and new pink tennis shoes and a lunchbox with a picture of Wonder Woman on it. Having all those new things made her happy.

But she was scared about not knowing anyone and making mistakes and stuff like that. Mom drove us to school the first day, so she would be certain Bernice got to the right classroom. I think Mom was as nervous as Bernice!

Mom insisted that I go with them, so I'd know where to meet Bernice after school. As if I didn't already know the school like the back of my hand. But it's hard to explain things like that to a nervous mother. The

good thing was Mom said Rick could ride with us.

On the way to school Bernice asked Rick and me a million dumb questions.

"Do you think we'll get to paint today? Can first-graders play on the big kids' playground? Do you think I'll make friends?"

Rick poked me in the arm. "Does she have to come with us every day?"

I rolled my eyes and nodded. Rick doesn't have a little sister, so he doesn't understand these things.

"Well, can't you shut her up?" Rick said.

I pointed to the rearview mirror. I could see Mom glaring. I made motions for Rick to keep his mouth shut or else!

Rick groaned. I was feeling pretty miserable myself. This school year was not getting off to a great start.

When we got to school, Mom and I took Bernice to her classroom and turned her over to her teacher, Mrs. Wilson.

Mom had to tell Mrs. Wilson all about Bernice. Like how she was allergic to shrimp and how much she liked to draw pictures and stuff like that. I didn't see how Bernice's allergy was so important. After all, how many first-graders eat shrimp on the first day of school? But Mrs. Wilson tried to listen patiently while Mom and three other parents all told life-and-death stories about their kids.

First-graders are sure noisy. A bunch of them were bouncing around like kangaroos and yelling at each other. Two other kids were crying because their mothers had to leave. Mrs. Wilson had her hands full.

I looked at Bernice. Her eyes were big and round. I could tell she was kind of scared.

"Look at those crybabies," I whispered. "You aren't a crybaby, Bernice."

She shook her head.

"Okay, have fun," I said. "I'll see you after school."

I had a pretty good day, *as far as first days go*. My teacher, Mr. Dumbarton, seemed okay, but I had my doubts. You could tell he was a pro when it came to fourth-graders.

He smiled and joked a lot, but I knew he was just waiting for one of us to get out of line. Then, boom! I had a feeling that after the first couple days, he'd get tough.

After school I wanted to go to the park with the other kids for a game of ball, but I had to go get Bernice. My friend Rick said, "Too bad. We're going to get chocolate slushees afterwards. Well, I'll see you tomorrow morning." And he grinned.

I said, "See you." All the way to Bernice's classroom I wished I were an only child like Rick.

Bernice was waiting for me outside her classroom like Mom had told her to. She sure didn't look like the same kid we'd dropped off that morning. She had blue paint smeared on one cheek and a scraped knee. Her hair ribbon was untied, and she'd torn the pocket on her new dress.

"What happened to you?" I said.

Her lower lip came out, a bad sign. "I hate first grade," she said. "Everything went wrong. I broke three crayons, and I spilled my milk and everyone laughed. And I didn't make any new friends."

That night at dinner, Bernice announced that she was quitting school. I saw Dad clap his hand over his mouth, and I knew he was trying hard not to laugh. Mom looked like she does when one of us breaks a dish or the sink backs up.

"Honey, you can't quit," Mom said. "You haven't given first grade much of a chance."

"Yes, I have, " Bernice wailed. "I hate it. You said I'd make new friends and I haven't."

"Why don't you try it for a few more days," Dad said. "You just need to get to know the other kids a little better."

"That's right," Mom said with a cheerful smile. "Just a few more days and everything will be fine."

But everything wasn't fine. A whole week went by and Bernice hadn't made any friends in her class. "There's got to be someone in school you like," I said.

Bernice shook her head. "I want a friend who's just like me," she said. "I want a friend who likes to do the same things I do and eat the same stuff I eat and who won't laugh if I make mistakes."

I didn't say anything because I figured that was impossible. No two kids are exactly alike. But that was before Buster showed up!

CHAPTER 2

The following Monday morning, Bernice got sick.

We were all rushing around trying to get ready. Dad couldn't find his car keys, and he was getting mad. Mom burned the French toast, and that made her mad. Bernice hogged the bathroom, which made me mad.

Finally Mom called us to the table. Everyone came, including Rufus, our dog, because he loves burned French toast. There was still no sign of Bernice.

"Where's your sister?" Mom said. "How come you haven't combed your hair, Danny?"

"Bernice is in the bathroom," I said. "She won't let me in, so don't blame me if we're late for school."

I slipped my toast under the table to Rufus. Then I looked up and saw Dad watching me. Oops, I thought, here it comes. Dad just winked, and I saw his toast disappear under the table, too.

"Bernice, hurry up," Mom yelled.

"I can't. I'm sick," Bernice wailed from the bathroom.

Mom ran down the hall and rattled the bathroom door. "Unlock this door," she said. "What's wrong with you?"

"I've got spots!" Bernice said. "Awful spots all over my face and arms and maybe on my tongue."

Dad and I tore down the hall after Mom. By that time, Mom had gotten Bernice to unlock the bathroom door.

Mom was standing in the doorway. Bernice was on the other side of the room, holding a towel over the bottom part of her face. But we could see the spots and sure enough, it looked like they were all over her.

"Oh, no!" Mom groaned. "Not chicken pox."

"Everyone stay away from me," Bernice wailed. "I'm catching."

"Not you, dummy," I said, "it's chicken pox that's catching."

Dad walked over to Bernice, in spite of the danger, and looked at her close up. Then he rubbed one of the spots. It smeared. "Looks like Magic Marker to me," he said.

"Magic Marker?" Mom stormed across the room and leaned over till she was almost nose-to-nose with Bernice.

"Magic Marker?" I howled. I ran down the hall to my room. Sure enough, my new set of markers was gone. "Bernice, you big dummy!" I yelled.

When I got back to the bathroom, Mom was scrubbing Bernice's face with a wash cloth to get off the spots she'd painted on, and Dad was teasing her about having a terrible disease called paint pox.

"Bernice, why did you do such a silly thing?" Mom said crossly.

"I don't want to go to school!" Bernice wailed.

Mom looked at Dad and Dad looked at Mom and they both sighed.

Mom sat down on the edge of the tub and put her arms around Bernice. "It's going to get better," she said. "I promise."

"You say that every day," Bernice cried, "but it never does. Yesterday I broke three more crayons, and I think Mrs. Wilson hates me."

"Oh, I'm sure she doesn't hate you, honey," Mom said. "I'll tell you what. How about if I buy you a new box of crayons? Would that make you feel better?"

"And Twinkies for my lunch box?" Bernice snuffled with her head on Mom's shoulder.

Mom nodded.

"And no more peanut butter sandwiches?"

Mom sighed. "Okay."

"And a new Barbie doll?"

She was really pushing her luck. "No Barbie doll," Mom said firmly. She stood up and wiped Bernice's eyes. "Now get ready for school."

Mom went back to the kitchen to fix some French toast for Bernice.

Dad winked at us. "Don't worry," he told Bernice. "Things will get better. You'll see." Then he left to go hunt for his car keys.

Bernice said, "Danny, will I ever have a best friend at school?"

Believe it or not, I felt kind of sorry for her. School is tough enough even with a best friend.

"Sure you will," I said. "Isn't there anyone in your class you'd like to be friends with?"

Bernice shook her head. "There's a girl in my class named Melody. But I don't want her for a friend."

"Why not?"

"Because she already knows all her alphabet, and she can count to a hundred."

"So can you."

"She can add, too. And she has these pencils with her name on them in gold letters. And worst of all, she eats liverwurst sandwiches."

I understood how Bernice felt. How can you be friends with someone who likes liverwurst?

"Well, there's got to be some kid you'll get to know," I said. Then I had a brain storm. "Don't forget, sometimes kids transfer in after school starts. So maybe a new kid will start school this week, and that's the kid who'll be your best friend. But if you don't go to school, Bernice, you'll never know."

Her eyes got big and round, and I could see she was thinking this one over. Then she smiled. "Okay, Danny, I'll go to school."

I was very proud of myself. I'd done what Mom and Dad couldn't do. I'd solved the problem of getting Bernice to want to go to school.

CHAPTER 3

That afternoon when I picked Bernice up at her classroom, I could tell she was really excited about something. She started jumping up and down the moment she saw me. "Danny, Danny! Guess what! I made a friend."

"Well, that's great," I said. "Who's your new friend?"

"Her name is Buster," Bernice said. "She's just like me!"

Oh, no, I thought. Two Bernice Penworthys in the same universe?

"She and I are best friends," Bernice said, skipping along.

"What did you say her name was?"

"Buster. That's just her nickname. Today we all got to tell the teacher if we wanted to be called by our nicknames. And Buster's nickname is Buster. Isn't that neat?"

"Bernice," I said, "Buster sounds like a boy's name. What kind of girl would have a name like that?"

Bernice was too excited to answer any questions. She just kept talking about Buster. "Oh, Danny, she chews her pencils, and she hates liverwurst sandwiches. Just like me. We're going to be best friends forever."

I was glad Bernice had finally made a friend. But when she told Mom and Dad, Mom said, "Buster?" like she didn't believe that could be a girl's name, not even a nickname.

"What is Buster's real name?" Dad said.

Bernice shrugged. "Buster says her real name is ugly and she hates it. You know what she wants to be when she grows up? A mud wrestler."

Mom gave a little shudder.

"What does Melody think of Buster?" I asked.

"Melody hates Buster. That's because Melody is stuck-up. You know what? Melody doesn't have to wear tennis shoes to school. She has black patent Mary Janes."

I could see Mom frowning a little like she was thinking. Then she said, "Would you like black patent Mary Janes?"

I knew just what was going on in Mom's head. Mom wanted Bernice to have a friend, but she didn't want Bernice to be friends with someone who wanted to be a mud wrestler. Secretly she hoped that Bernice would start to like Melody who wore black patent Mary Janes.

Bernice said she would love a pair of black patent Mary Janes. So Mom said on Saturday they'd go shopping. I said, "Hey, what about me?"

Dad said, "You want a pair of black patent Mary Janes?"

"No," I said. "I want a new skateboard."

Mom said, "Now, Danny!"

I said, "Bernice gets new shoes. Why can't I have a skateboard?"

Just because Mom wanted Bernice to be more like Melody and less like Buster, it wasn't fair for her to buy something for my dumb sister and nothing for me. But that's the way it is when you have a little sister. They always get spoiled.

Everything worked out okay, though, because while Mom and Bernice went shopping, Dad took me to a ball game. We ate so many hot dogs and bags of peanuts and cotton candy, we almost got sick. It was great.

The Mary Janes didn't make any difference. Bernice wore them almost every day, but she still hung around Buster. And every day she talked about Buster. It was Buster this and Buster that until I thought Mom and Dad were going to explode.

I had to admit that Buster sounded like an interesting kid. She managed to get into more trouble than anyone I knew. She talked when she was supposed to be listening. She was out of her seat when she was supposed to be doing her work. When the class fingerpainted, she was the only kid who got paint on the teacher's favorite sweater.

"Oh, goodness," Mom said. "Poor Mrs. Wilson. I bet she wanted to strangle Buster."

"Mrs. Wilson doesn't understand," Bernice said. "Buster doesn't mean to get into trouble. She just has so many great ideas. I'm glad she's my friend."

"Well, be careful," Mom said. "Sounds to me like if you hang around Buster, you could get into trouble, too."

That night when we were doing the dishes, Bernice said, "Danny, did Rick ever get you in trouble?"

"Well —" There were a few times when Rick and I had had to stay after school, but luckily Mom and Dad had never found out.

"I don't understand why Mom and Dad don't like Buster," Bernice said.

"Maybe you should just tell them about the good things Buster does, not all the bad things," I said.

Bernice thought about that. Then she said, "I guess you're right."

I couldn't believe it. My own sister had agreed with me. This was the second time I'd solved a problem for her.

"She does a few good things, doesn't she?" I asked. "I mean, she can't be all bad."

"Of course," Bernice said. "No one is all bad. You're not all bad, are you?"

"Of course not," I said.

"I'm not all bad," Bernice said.

I had to agree with that, too. Then I said, "What about Melody? Isn't she ever bad?"

"Oh, yuck!" said Bernice. "Never!"

CHAPTER 4

By now I was dying to get a look at this kid Buster.

When I listened to Mom talk about Buster, I pictured a kid with horns and fangs. When I listened to Bernice talk about her, I pictured a little mud wrestler with a halo and wings. I couldn't wait to see what this kid really looked like. But every time I went to pick Bernice up at her classroom, Buster had already left.

One day at school I finally got my chance. It was just after recess, and Mr. Dumbarton asked me to take a note to Mrs. Wilson's class. I said, "Yes, sir," and grabbed the note and ran.

But as soon as I was out of sight, I slowed

down. I didn't want to get back to class too soon. This was math period, and Mr. Dumbarton always collected our homework first thing. I hadn't done last night's homework, so I figured if I took my time, maybe when I got back, he'd have forgotton about my paper. Then I could do it at lunch recess and sneak it into the homework papers on his desk. So I stopped for a drink of water and retied my shoes, and then I decided to take the long way around by the little kids' playground. There were big windows in the classrooms that looked out over the playground. I figured I could sneak up and peak in Mrs. Wilson's window and catch sight of Buster.

But right at the edge of the playground, I heard someone call my name.

I looked around but didn't see anyone.

"Danny!" There it was again. "Up here!"

I looked up and my teeth almost fell out. There was my stupid sister, sitting up in a tree!

"Bernice, what are you doing up there?" I gasped.

"I'm stuck," she wailed. "I can't get down. And the bell rang and I'm late and I'm going to get in trouble."

"I'll say," I grumbled.

If anyone happened to be passing by and saw us, Bernice wasn't going to be the only one in trouble. Still, I couldn't just leave her there. "Hang on," I said, "I'll come up and help you down."

I grabbed the lowest branch and started climbing. Bernice was like a kitten who tears up a tree and then can't get back down. Every time she looked at the ground, she got scared and started to whimper.

"Don't look down!" I told her.

The only way I could get her down was to make her close her eyes and wrap her arms around the trunk. Then I told her where to put her hands and feet.

"Put your right foot down on the next branch, Bernice. Don't be scared. It's only six inches away. No, dummy, not your left foot, your right foot."

On the way down I scraped my elbow, and Bernice kicked me in the face. But I finally got her to the ground. Then I had to get her into the classroom without the teacher seeing her.

I said, "What were you doing up in that tree anyway? Don't you know that kids aren't supposed to climb trees on the school grounds?"

"It was Buster's idea," Bernice said. "She wanted to hide from Melody because Melody's such a pest."

"You mean your great friend Buster left you stuck up in that tree?"

Bernice stuck her lower lip out, and I changed the subject fast.

By that time, we'd reached Bernice's classroom. Luckily for us, all the kids were getting into their reading circle. There were so many kids running around that Mrs. Wilson didn't see Bernice duck behind me and sneak in fast. I waited till she melted into the group, then I took the note to Mrs. Wilson.

While Mrs. Wilson was reading it, I looked around the room. I was dying to see Buster. In my mind, I kind of imagined she had short curly hair and freckles and a couple front teeth missing.

The trouble was, there were about half a dozen little girls who looked like that, including my own sister. I couldn't figure out which one was Buster. I did see Melody. I knew it had to be Melody because she was the only girl in the room without scabs on her knees, paint on her face, or dirty hands. Bernice was right. Melody looked like a goody-goody jerk.

By the time I got back back to my own classroom, the students were halfway through a pop quiz. Mr. Dumbarton was really mad because I was so late. He hadn't forgotten about my homework, either. When he found out I didn't have it with me, he told me I could stay in at lunch recess to do the homework and stay after school to take the quiz.

I was mad! I figured the whole thing was Buster's fault. After all, if she hadn't talked Bernice into climbing that tree, none of this ever would have happened.

By the time Mr. Dumbarton let me go after school, it was really late. I ran over to Bernice's classroom. No Bernice! I went out to the playground. No Bernice. I searched the whole school for my sister, but I couldn't find her anywhere.

CHAPTER 5

Now I was really scared. What had that little creep done with herself? I thought maybe she'd gone to the park. So I went to the park. No Bernice. Then I thought maybe she'd stopped off to buy a chocolate slushee. Wrong again.

When I got home, I found that Bernice had walked home by herself. She was so proud of what she'd done that she had called Mom from our neighbor's house to tell her she didn't have a key to let herself in. Mom was so upset that she'd taken off from work and come right home. Mom was ready to kill me.

"Do you realize what could have happened to your little sister on the way home from school? What if she'd gotten lost?

What if someone had kidnapped her?"

I really couldn't imagine my sister being kidnapped. I mean, who would want Bernice?

"It wasn't my fault," I said. "I didn't know I'd have to stay after school."

"I told you before school started that you have to take care of your sister," Mom said. "You are grounded, Daniel Penworthy. For a week! Maybe that will help you remember to do your homework, so you don't get kept after school and Bernice isn't stranded. Understand?"

She stomped out of the room.

"Thanks a lot," I said to Bernice. "How come you walked home alone?"

"I didn't mean to get you in trouble," Bernice said. "It was Buster's idea. She knows the way to my house by heart."

I stared at my sister. "Buster knows where you live?"

"Uh-huh."

"You mean Buster lives around here?"

Bernice nodded.

That gave me a great idea. If Buster knew the way home, Bernice could walk home from school with her! And that meant I could walk with Rick. All I had to do was wait until Mom calmed down.

I had lots of time to wait. A whole week. I guess toward the end, Mom was sorry she'd grounded me for so long. "Danny Penworthy, get out of that refrigerator. Turn off the TV. And stop bugging that poor dog. Don't you have something to do?"

I shook my head. "I'm grounded, remember?"

I decided it would be smarter to tell Dad my great plan first. I even agreed to spend a Saturday morning helping him clean out the garage. That gave us a chance to talk.

"I bet Bernice would much rather walk home with one of her friends," I said. "And Buster knows the way, too, so they can't get lost."

Dad rolled his eyes. "Buster!" he said.

"Buster's her best friend," I said.

"I wonder about that kid," Dad said. "She

must be pretty independent. I wonder what her family is like."

"Maybe she's the oldest child," I said. "I'm the oldest and you and Mom used to let me walk home by myself when I was Bernice's age."

Dad smiled. "I guess we did, didn't we," he said. "Maybe it's because you're a boy and Bernice is a little girl."

"That's not fair." I said. "You and Mom said boys and girls should have the same rights and the same responsibilities."

"We did say that, didn't we," Dad said. "Well, I'll talk it over with your mother, and we'll talk to Bernice about it, too. I sure would like to meet this Buster."

"Me, too," I said. "Maybe we could get Bernice to have her over to play some time."

"Good idea," Dad said. "Any kid who wants to be a mud wrestler must be one interesting kid." And he grinned.

Dad talked to Mom about Bernice walking home from school with Buster. At first Mom was against the idea. "Do you realize we don't know Buster's real name?" Mom said. "We don't know where that child lives or even her phone number?"

I'd never thought about that before, but it seemed kind of silly to me.

"There's a lot we don't know about Buster," I said. "Like what her parents do for a living. How many kids are in the family. Or even if she's had all her shots." I was joking, but Mom was in no mood for jokes. She looked horrified, especially when I got to the part about the shots.

"Take it easy," Dad said. "Danny's only kidding. I think we ought to give Bernice a chance. Sooner or later, we'll meet Buster and her family."

Mom finally agreed.

Bernice thought it was a great idea. It made her feel so grown up.

Mom figured out how long it would take Bernice to get home from school. She gave Bernice a key to the house, pinned to the inside of her clothes so she wouldn't lose it. She made Bernice go over all the safety rules, like don't talk to strangers and don't cross the street against the light and don't stop to play.

"You come straight home," Mom said. "You come right in the house and call me at work." Bernice listened to all this very carefully. She promised to do what Mom said.

Everything went fine for the rest of the week, so Mom began to relax.

I felt great. Now I had my freedom back. Rick and I walked home together and did the things we'd done before Bernice started school. We went by the park to shoot some baskets, and afterwards, we bought chocolate slushees and corn nuts.

I was ready to forgive Buster for getting me in trouble. But then, she did it again!

CHAPTER 6

One afternoon when I got home from school, I found the front door was locked. I could hear the phone ringing. I couldn't figure out why Bernice didn't answer it. I unlocked the door and tore into the house.

"Bernice!" I yelled as I ran for the phone. There was no answer.

I grabbed the phone. "Hello?"

There was a lot of shouting on the other end. I thought maybe it was a wrong number until I realized it was Mom calling. She sure sounded upset.

"Daniel Penworthy, where have you been? I've called and called and no one answers."

"Uh —"

"Where is your sister? You put her on the line this minute!"

"Uh —"

"I'm really angry with her. She's supposed to call me the minute she gets home. She should have been home twenty minutes ago."

"Uh —"

"I knew I shouldn't have let her walk home by herself. It's all Buster's fault. I just bet those girls are outside playing. I've told Bernice over and over, when you get home from school . . . ."

Mom went on and on. It's a good thing, too, because it gave me time to take a quick look through the kitchen window. Bernice wasn't in the backyard, and I knew she wasn't out front. Maybe those idiot girls were in her room playing with her Barbies.

Thank goodness for long phone cords. I dragged the phone down the hall as far as it would go. I stuck the phone inside my jacket so Mom wouldn't hear me hollering. "Bernice!"

There was no answer. In fact, the house was really quiet. Too quiet! Then I realized what was wrong. Bernice wasn't home. That's when I panicked.

I put the phone back to my ear. Mom was still carrying on about how Bernice and I never listened to a word she said and how if she had acted like that when she was a kid, her mother would have grounded her for life. I think she was about to start her Kids-Today-Have-No-Respect speech when I heard the front door open.

I stuffed the phone back under my jacket and yelled, "Bernice! Is that you?"

She ran into the kitchen looking really scared. "Get over here," I ordered. "Mom's on the phone."

Bernice's eyes were as round as saucers. "Is she mad?"

"Mad? Oh, no, she's not mad. She'll probably just ground you for life."

Bernice groaned. I saw that lower lip come out and that was the last straw. "Bernice, if you cry, I'll kill you," I said.

"This is no time to be a crybaby. You have to talk to Mom."

"What am I going to say?" she wailed.

I slapped the phone into Bernice's hand. "You figure it out," I said as I went to get myself a cookie.

"Hi, Mom," she said in a shaky voice.

I could hear Mom's voice coming out of that phone clear across the room. I heard Bernice say, "I'm sorry I didn't call. I forgot."

That's a kid's favorite excuse. That and "I don't know." I guess Mom bought it because Bernice said, "Uh-huh" and "Huh-uh" a lot. Then her lower lip came out. Her eyes filled with tears. Here we go, I thought.

She hung up the phone and started to cry. "Well?" I said.

"I'm grounded all day Saturday. I can't go out and play."

"You'll live," I said. "I've been grounded lots. It's no big deal, Bernice. In fact, you're really lucky that Mom only grounded you for one day. I guess that's because she didn't realize you weren't home."

Bernice hung her head.

"So where were you, dummy? How come you're late?"

"I had to stay after school."

I whistled, which is hard to do with a mouthful of cookie crumbs. "What did you do?"

"It wasn't just me," Bernice wailed. "It was everyone at our table. We had to stay after school because of Buster."

"You're kidding, what did Buster do?"

"She was just being helpful," Bernice said. "She was trying to help Melody with her arithmetic because Buster knew the answers but Melody didn't. And Buster saw that Melody didn't know, so she told her. But Melody got mad and told Buster to leave her alone, and I got mad at Melody and told her she was stupid and stuckup. Then the other kids yelled at me to stop yelling at Melody, and the teacher got mad and yelled at everybody."

I whistled again. I said, "Melody the Superkid yelled at Buster? I thought Melody was never bad."

"Buster was only trying to help Melody," Bernice said. "Everybody thinks Melody is such hot stuff. Even Melody thinks she's hot. I can't stand that girl."

"Look," I said, "I understand why you don't like Melody, but helping Buster got you in a lot of trouble. You'd better be careful, Bernice."

Bernice looked shocked. "Buster is my best friend," she said. "My best friend in the whole world."

"I know," I said, "but — "

"What about you and Rick?" she asked. "Isn't he your best friend?" Would you stop hanging around Rick if you got in trouble because he got in trouble trying to help someone?"

"When Rick gets in trouble it's not because he's trying to help someone," I said.

"Well, Buster does. She likes to help people. And she has great ideas, too." Bernice folded her arms over her chest and glared at me. "So there!"

I didn't say another word. It seemed to me that Buster was like a case of chicken pox. But I knew I couldn't make Bernice see that. She'd have to find out for herself.

CHAPTER 7

Bernice didn't tell Mom about having to stay after school. Neither did I. I guess Mom would never have found out except that one day she took the afternoon off from work to take the dog to the vet and clean the refrigerator. That just happened to be a day when Bernice had to stay after school again.

When I got home, Mom was having a fit. "Where is your sister?" she said.

"Why ask me? I don't keep track of Bernice," I said.

Then I was sorry I'd said it like that, because if I didn't watch my mouth, Mom might make me go back to walking Bernice home each day. "Maybe she went to Buster's house," I said, trying to help.

Mom looked horrified. Like I'd just suggested that Bernice had gone down into the sewer.

"Relax, Mom, Bernice says Buster lives right here in the neighborhood," I said. "Why don't I go look for her?"

Just then the front door flew open and Bernice rushed in. I couldn't tell if Mom was going to hug her or yell at her. Finally she did both.

"Where have you been?" Mom yelled, grabbing Bernice in a big hug. "I've been worried sick about you."

"I had to stay after school again." Bernice said. Then her eyes got round, and she put her hand over her mouth.

"Oops," I said.

Mom looked shocked. "What do mean, you had to stay after school *again*? You mean, this isn't the first time?" Her voice was getting higher.

"It wasn't my fault," Bernice said.

"Whose fault was it?" Mom said.

"It was nobody's fault. Buster was just trying to be helpful, but Mrs. Wilson didn't understand. She never understands."

Mom groaned. She sank down on the sofa and pointed to the cushion right next to her. "I think you'd better tell me all about it," she said.

"Do I have to?" Bernice said.

"Do you want to live?" I said with a grin.

"That's enough, Daniel," Mom said. "All right, Bernice, from the beginning."

"Well, it started with the ants," Bernice said. "They were crawling out of a crack in the ant farm, and Buster thought it would be a good idea to put them in the paper clip box in Mrs. Wilson's desk until somebody could fix the ant farm."

Mom looked sick.

"It was a good idea." Bernice said, "until that dumb Melody went to get a paper clip and got an ant bite instead. Boy, did she yell." Bernice giggled, and I couldn't help grinning. Mom was looking sicker.

"So how come you had to stay after school

if all this was Buster's idea?" Mom said.

"Because Buster told me to put the ants in the paper clip box," said Bernice.

That was the last straw. Mom blew her top! "Bernice Jane Penworthy, you have to stop hanging around that Buster," Mom said. "Do you hear me?"

Mom only calls us by our whole names when she's really upset. Bernice knew better than to argue. She just went quietly to her room.

I decided it was time for me to have a talk with her. I was tired of Mom being mad, because when Mom is mad at Bernice, she always says to me, "And what about you, Daniel? Have you finished your homework? Did you clean your room?"

I went to Bernice's door and knocked. No answer, so I opened the door. She was sitting on the bed, sulking.

"You aren't being smart about all this," I told her. "If you want to be friends with Buster, you've got to stop talking about her."

"You said not to talk about the bad things she did."

"What do you call putting ants in the paper clip box, dummy?"

"I thought it was a good idea," Bernice said. "Buster was only trying to help. Don't you think it was a nice thing to do?"

"Not if you got in trouble for it. If you can keep out of trouble for a while, maybe Mom will forget what she said about you and Buster not hanging around each other."

"That's a good idea," Bernice said slowly.

Was I hearing right? This was the third time Bernice had listened to me.

I couldn't resist adding, "And maybe, someday, if you and Buster don't get into any more trouble, Mom and Dad will let you have Buster come over to play. I bet after they meet her, they'll like her and — What?"

Bernice had a really weird look on her face. "That's a terrible idea," she gasped. "If you tell anyone, I'll feed soap flakes to your guppies!"

That made me mad. "You do and I'll shave all the hair off your Barbie dolls," I yelled.

We started throwing things at each other until Mom sent me to my room.

That's when I started wondering about Buster. How come Bernice didn't want Mom and Dad to meet her? What was wrong with her? I knew she was a troublemaker, but Bernice was acting so weird, I figured there had to be something else really strange about Buster. Like maybe Buster had two heads or green fur on her toes or something.

I almost laughed out loud. They'd never let a kid with green furry toes go to school. No, it had to be something simple, like maybe she never took a bath or she ate worms at recess. That figured. Leave it to my sister to be best friends with the class weirdo.

CHAPTER 8

It was almost Halloween. Rick and I had big plans.

Mr. Dumbarton had turned out to be a real jerk. Ever since the time he made me stay after school, he was always on my case.

It's true I wasn't his best student. It's true I didn't do my homework as often as he wanted. But that didn't make me a monster.

Besides, it was Rick who put the toad in his desk, not me. Mr. Dumbarton blamed me anyhow and in front of the whole class, too. He said that since I liked toads so much, I might as well do a report on one. A thousand words and I couldn't use the word *toad*. I had to use some fancy scientific

word, *Bufo vulgaris,* which he said meant common toad.

It was due that day. That meant I had to miss recess to work on it *and* stay after school, too. It was one of the worst days of my life.

I was miserable. Rick felt really sorry that he'd gotten me in so much trouble. Not sorry enough to tell Mr. Dumbarton the truth, but sorry enough to help me get even.

We found out where Mr. Dumbarton lived, and we set a date for getting revenge. Halloween!

"We could soap his windows," I said.

Rick shook his head. "Everyone does that. We need to think of something really awful."

"Wrap toilet paper around his house?"

"Where are we going to get that much toilet paper?" said Rick.

"Okay, you think of something," I said.

Rick grinned. "We could throw eggs at his door."

I shook my head. "That's what a lot of people do on Halloween," I said. "I think we should do something really different."

We were quiet for a few minutes, thinking. Then Rick said, "How about if we shave his dog?"

"Seems kind of mean," I said. "What do you have against his dog?"

"Nothing," said Rick. "Only I figure his dog must be really dumb."

"Why do you say that?"

"Because it doesn't even bite Mr. Dumdum." Rick laughed.

"Get serious," I said. "Dogs aren't supposed to bite their owners."

Rick sighed. "I was only joking," he said.

It was hard work thinking up mean tricks to play on Mr. Dumbarton. And time was getting short.

Luckily for everyone, Bernice took my advice. She stopped talking about Buster. It was almost as if Buster didn't exist. Mom was really glad of that. But once in a while, she would ask Bernice about Buster. I guess she wanted to make sure there'd be no more trouble. "How's Buster?" Mom would ask.

Bernice would just shrug and say, "Okay."

One afternoon Bernice brought a note home from school. It had Mom's name on the outside, but Bernice gave it to Dad instead.

"My teacher says you have to sign it so she knows you saw it," Bernice said. "It's not really important. You can sign it, and I'll tell you what it says later."

"If it's for Mom, why are you giving it to me?" Dad said.

"I didn't want to bother Mom. She's busy. You really don't need to read it, Daddy."

She was hopping from one foot to the other, and she sounded a little scared. Uh-oh, I thought, what's going on?

Dad said, "Hmm," under his breath. He opened the note and read it. Then he said, "I think we'd better bother Mom."

He showed the note to Mom and she read it out loud. It said:

Dear Mrs. Penworthy,

Please do not send Super Glue to school anymore. I prefer to have the students use washable white paste for school projects.

Sincerely yours,
Mrs. Wilson

Mom frowned. "What's this all about, Bernice? I didn't send Super Glue to school. Did I?" She looked at Dad. He just shrugged.

"No, but Mrs. Wilson thinks you did," Bernice said. "She made a mistake, that's all. You can sign the note now."

She handed Mom a pen. She was being very helpful. Too helpful.

"Wait a minute," Mom said. "Did you tell Mrs. Wilson it was a mistake?"

"She was busy," Bernice said. "I didn't want to bother her."

"Who brought the Super Glue to school?" Dad asked.

"Buster did."

"Oh, really?" said Dad. "And what happened with the Super Glue?"

"Nothing," Bernice said.

That's another favorite answer with kids. I was really proud of Bernice. She was learning fast.

"Well, something must have happened," Mom said. "Otherwise, Mrs. Wilson wouldn't have sent me this note."

Bernice sighed. "It was Buster's idea. And it was a great idea, too. We had to glue macaroni on construction paper to make pictures for art. But paste doesn't glue stuff very well and the macaroni always falls off and then the picture looks ugly. So Buster said we ought to use Super Glue. I thought that was a great idea."

"But Mrs. Wilson didn't think so, I guess," said Dad.

"Did you ask Mrs. Wilson if you could use Super Glue?" Mom asked.

"Mrs. Wilson was busy, and we didn't want to bother her," Bernice said. "But then Buster forgot to clean off the table when we finished and when we put our chairs up, they got stuck to the table. And now the custodian has to unstick them."

"Oh, good grief," Mom said. "I thought you weren't hanging around Buster anymore."

"Mom, we sit at the same table," Bernice said.

"Well, that does it!" Mom said. "I'm going

to have a little talk with Mrs. Wilson. I want you moved to another table."

Bernice turned white as a sheet. Honest! I'd never seen her look like that, not even when she had the flu. Then she burst into tears and ran out of the room.

Mom said, "Oh, dear!"

Dad said, "Maybe we're being a little unfair."

Mom said, "I didn't mean to upset her, but I've had it with Buster. I've had it right up to here."

Dad said, "I know, but we can't choose Bernice's friends for her."

Mom said, "I just don't understand why she can't be friends with Melody. Melody sounds like such a nice little girl."

Parents are so strange. Sometimes it's hard to believe they were ever kids.

I said, "I know why Bernice doesn't want to be friends with Melody."

They both looked at me.

"Why?" they both said at the same time.

"Because Melody is a dumb little jerk

who eats liverwurst sandwiches and tattles. Would you want Bernice to be friends with someone like that?"

Mom groaned. "Go do your homework, Daniel."

CHAPTER 9

On my way down the hall, I heard Bernice in her room. It sounded like she was destroying it. I opened the door a crack to see what she was doing. What a mess!

I ran into her room and grabbed her arm just before she threw her Barbie house against the mirror. "What are you doing?"

"I'm uncleaning my room," she yelled. "I'm going to flush all my doll clothes down the toilet, and I'm going to throw my Barbies away. Then I'm going to run away from home and never come back. Let go of me!"

"Not until you calm down," I said. "Why do you want to run away from home? Because Mom said you couldn't sit at Buster's table? Get real, Bernice. Mom doesn't know what you do at school. You and Buster can still be friends. You can play together at recess, and you can eat lunch together and — "

Bernice tried to pull her arm loose. "Let me go," she hollered. "I'm going to run away, and you can't stop me."

Her face was all red and she was panting. I'd never seen her so upset.

"Don't worry," I said. "Why should I try to stop you? If you run away, then there will be more for me. I just want you to think about what you're doing. So you get it right the first time and don't want to come back home."

"What do you mean, more for you?" Bernice said.

"You know. More ice cream, more Twinkies, not having to share the TV with you. Have you figured out where you're going to live?" I said.

Bernice stopped struggling. "I don't know."

"See what I mean? You don't have a plan. Now think about it. Would you like to live in the park?"

Bernice loved the park. She thought about

that for a minute and then she nodded. "That's a great idea. Thanks, Danny."

"Glad I could help," I said. "Of course, at night it gets scary because it's so dark. I bet there are lots of wild animals that live in the park and only come out at night. You know, bears and wolves and things. Would that bother you?"

Bernice nodded. "I don't want to live in the park."

My plan was working. She was beginning to think twice about running away.

"I bet you want to go live with Buster," I said.

Bernice shook her head.

"Why not? Just because Mom and Dad don't want you to be friends with her? If you're going to run away, you don't care what they think, do you?"

Bernice sniffled. "Yes, I do," she said.

"Have you ever been to Buster's house?" I asked.

To my surprise, Bernice nodded. That was news to me. I wondered if Mom and Dad knew.

"What's her house like?" I said.

Bernice shrugged. "I don't know. It's just a house."

"Is it big or little, messy or clean?"

Bernice thought about that. "I guess it's like our house."

"Did you meet her parents? Are they nice?"

Bernice shrugged again. "They're just parents."

I was getting frustrated. If Bernice had said that Buster's house was a dump and her parents were monsters, I could understand. But the whole family sounded pretty ordinary.

By now Bernice had calmed down. She had quit yelling and throwing things, and her face wasn't so red.

"You still want to run away?" I said.

She nodded. "One of these days. After I have a plan."

That really confused me. I was so sure I'd talked her out of it. "Just because Mom's going to have you moved to another table?"

"Danny, you don't understand anything," Bernice wailed. "If Mom and Dad ever meet Buster, they're going to ground me for life. No, worse, they'll kill me."

"I don't get it," I said. "What's so terrible about this girl? You make her sound like a monster. How can you be friends with someone like that?"

I thought about the green furry toes. Maybe I hadn't been wrong after all.

"I can't tell you," Bernice said.

"Bernice, it's me, Danny. You can tell me anything."

"I can?"

"Trust me."

"You promise? Cross your heart and hope to die?"

I crossed my heart. I held my breath. I was finally going to learn the terrible truth about Buster!

"Daaaannnnyyyy! Rick's on the phone!" Mom yelled from the kitchen.

I groaned. I could have strangled Rick for calling me just then.

CHAPTER 10

Rick had thought of a way for us to get old Dumdum Dumbarton on Halloween.

Rick's plan was brilliant. Mr. Dumbarton's yard was his pride and joy. He kept it looking perfect. There was a nice green lawn and flower beds and around the whole thing was a big hedge.

Mr. Dumbarton kept that hedge perfectly trimmed. There wasn't a leaf or a branch out of place. He fertilized that hedge and watered it until it was the most beautiful shade of green you ever saw. It was a work of art.

Rick's plan was to spray paint the hedge. He figured we could buy some cans of purple and red paint and have a blast.

"It will be months before he gets that hedge back to normal," Rick laughed. "It'll drive him nuts."

"That's a great idea," I said. "I wish I'd thought of it. Where did you get such a great idea?"

"I don't know," Rick said.

"What do you mean, you don't know."

"My mom's calling me," he said. "I have to get off the phone." He hung up.

I was glad that Rick and I finally had a plan for Mr. Dumbarton. But I still didn't know the terrible truth about Buster.

I didn't get a chance to talk to Bernice again until after dinner when we were doing the dishes. By then she had changed her mind. "You might tell someone," she said.

"I promise I won't," I said. "Cross my heart, Bernice."

She shook her head, and nothing I said made her change her mind.

Meantime, something else was going on in school. We were getting ready for Open House.

Open House was held a week after Halloween. We all liked getting ready for Open House. It meant the teachers took class time to get the school fixed up, so they could show off for our parents. They made fancy bulletin boards to display our best papers. They made sure the fish tanks were cleaned out, and the drinking fountains weren't gunky. We did lots of science and art projects because parents like that kind of stuff.

It also meant that they skipped pop quizzes and gave us less homework. All except Mr. Dumbarton, of course. He just made us work harder. I could hardly wait for Halloween!

Rick and I were lucky. Halloween fell on a Friday. Our parents said we could stay out later than usual when we went trick-or-treating. That gave us plenty of time to paint Mr. Dumbarton's hedge.

After dinner Mom helped Bernice into her costume. Bernice was going trick-or-treating as a fairy princess. I was going as a vampire. I had fake fangs and everything.

"Mom, can I use ketchup for fake blood?" I asked.

Mom shuddered. "Okay, but don't get it on your clothes or it'll stain," she said.

Bernice began to whine. "How come I can't be a vampire?"

"Because you wanted to be a fairy princess," Mom said. "Now hold still so I can pin on your wings."

"How come you have to take me around?" Bernice said. "How come I can't go out with Danny and Rick?"

"Because," Mom said.

"Because why?"

"Because Rick and Danny are older," Mom said.

"It's not fair," Bernice whined. "You treat me like such a baby."

"You're not a baby," Mom said. "You're my beautiful little princess. Stop wiggling or your wings will be crooked."

I pulled my cloak up over my face. "Yes," I hissed. "Ifff you do not behave, I vill bite your neck and suck out all your blood."

Bernice stuck out her tongue.

Rick showed up dressed like a werewolf. He was carrying a big pillow case already loaded with candy.

"Wow," Dad said, when he saw the pillow case. "You're loaded down. When did you start trick-or-treating, at dawn?"

Rick just laughed. Then he grabbed my arm. "Come on," he said. "We have to go."

"Don't be late, boys. Don't go to anyone's house if you don't know the people. And don't eat any candy until Mom and I check it first."

"Yeah, Dad," I yelled as Rick dragged me out the door.

Once we were outside, he slowed down. "You know what's in the pillow case under the candy? Spray paint."

"Wow, neat!" I said. "What colors?"

"Red, orange, purple, and silver," Rick laughed. "Boy, is he going to be mad!"

We had to wait till the crowds of trick-or-treaters thinned out. Then we took out the spray paint and went to work. Did we have fun!

Rick figured out how to spray paint stripes and polka dots on the hedge. By the time we were finished, that hedge must have looked awful. We couldn't see it too well in the dark. We decided that on Saturday we'd ride by on our bikes to see how it looked.

But next morning Mom woke me up at

the crack of dawn. "Your teacher, Mr. Dumbarton, just phoned," she said between gritted teeth. "Do you know what he told me?"

I shrank down under the covers. "What?"

"Last night some kids spray painted his hedge. He's calling all the parents in the neighborhood to find out who did it."

About that time Dad and Bernice crowded into the doorway. Dad's hair was standing straight up all over his head and he looked sleepy.

"Who was that on the phone at this hour?" Dad said. He yawned.

Mom told him about Mr. Dumbarton's call. All of a sudden Dad didn't look sleepy anymore.

CHAPTER 11

They say that just before you die, your life flashes before your eyes. I don't know if it was my life or visions of what my parents would do to me if they found out the truth.

Bernice said, "Mom, I'm hungry."

"Not *now*, Bernice," Mom said. "Danny, do you know anything about Mr. Dumbarton's hedge?"

"Uh —"

"*Maahmm,* I'm huungrrry!"

"Not *now*," Mom said crossly.

"I'm hungry, too," Dad said. "Maybe we should deal with this little problem on a full stomach."

"Good idea," said Bernice. "I want Twinkies for breakfast. Can I have Twinkies for breakfast, Mom?" And before Mom could answer, Bernice made a dash for the kitchen.

Mom threw her hands up in the air. "Oh, I give up!" she said crossly. "Daniel, get up and get dressed. Bernice, leave the Twinkies alone!"

As yucky as it sounds, I could have kissed Bernice. She had saved my life, at least until after breakfast. And she'd given me some time to get rid of the paint under my fingernails. My hands never looked so clean as they did when I got to the kitchen.

When Mom is mad, we have great breakfasts. She takes her anger out on the pancake batter, I guess. Today she'd gone all out. We had pancakes, bacon, and hot chocolate with marshmallows on top. I knew she was really mad, but it was really good. The last meal of the condemned kid!

Dad said, "All right, son, time for the truth. Did you or didn't you spray paint Mr. Dumbarton's hedge?"

"I know who did it," Bernice said.

Mom and Dad turned to stare at her.

"How do you know? What do you know?" they said at the same time.

"It was Rick," Bernice said, licking syrup off her fingers. "But he had a good reason."

Mom and Dad turned and looked at me. "Is this true?" Mom said.

"Well—"

"You were with Rick last night," Mom said.

"Oh, Mom," Bernice giggled, "how can you think it was Danny? Does he have paint on his hands? Wouldn't Danny have paint on his hands if he spray painted a hedge? Red and orange and purple and silver fingers. Danny would look so gross."

Her giggles got louder, and she almost fell off the chair. It was the worst fake laugh I've ever heard. But I was grateful to her for trying.

"Wait a minute!" Dad said. "You seem to know a lot about this, young lady."

"Put your hands out, Danny," Mom said. She stared at them with a frown. "They look clean. Too clean."

"How do you know what colors they used?" Dad said to Bernice.

"Because!"

"That's not an answer," Mom said.

"Because Buster told me."

"*BUSTER?*" We all said it at the same time.

"It was Buster's idea," Bernice said. "See, Mr. Dumbarton did a really mean thing to

Danny. He blamed Danny for something that Danny didn't do. And then he punished him. It wasn't fair. So Rick decided to get even, only he couldn't think of a way. So Buster told him."

It got a little crazy after that. Mom and Dad made me tell them what Mr. Dumbarton had done to me. The story of *Bufo vulgaris* came out.

Then they asked me about my part in spray painting the hedge. Well, I can stretch the truth, and now and then I tell little white lies. But I just couldn't tell a whopper and blame it all on Rick.

I knew I was going to get punished. But I could see that Mom and Dad didn't think the toad report was fair, either. I had a feeling I'd get to live a little longer. At least until report cards were handed out.

Then Mom said, "Oh, that Buster! Where does she get these terrible ideas of hers?"

It was kind of funny, now that I thought about it. I could remember asking Rick where he'd gotten his great idea for spray painting the hedge. He acted like he didn't want to tell me. So Buster was the one behind it all. I had to give the weird kid credit. I still thought spray painting that hedge was pretty great. As for Bernice, sister or not, she'd saved my life.

"Okay, Bernice, give me Buster's phone number," Mom said. "I'm going to call her parents right now and have a talk with them."

"I don't know," Bernice said. "We don't talk on the phone." She looked pretty uncomfortable. I thought fast.

"Come on, Mom," I said. "Buster didn't do anything wrong. Giving Rick the idea wasn't wrong."

"That's right," Dad said, "and you and Rick should have known better." Then he said to Mom, "If Rick and Danny were dumb enough to do what Buster suggested, that's their problem, and they're the ones who have to make up for what they did to the teacher's hedge." Dad gave me a stern look.

"Can I go watch cartoons?" Bernice said.

Mom nodded and Bernice grabbed a handful of marshmallows to suck on while she watched TV. Then she headed for the family room. At the door she stopped and turned to grin at me.

I grinned back and winked.

CHAPTER 12

Finally the great night arrived. Open House. We all hurried to eat dinner and get dressed up. All of us except Bernice. She dawdled at the table, and she dawdled getting dressed.

Mom said, "Hurry up, Bernice, or we'll be late!"

I heard Bernice whisper, "Good!"

I knew why Bernice didn't want to go. Chances were, tonight we'd finally meet the famous Buster!

It felt strange to be going to school at night. The school looked strange, too, with all the lights on in the classrooms and people going from class to class while it was dark outside.

First we went to see my classroom. My

parents were finally going to meet Mr. Dumbarton, but I didn't care. Rick and I had already been given our punishment for the hedge trick. We had to spend every Saturday for a month cleaning Mr. Dumbarton's yard. I was glad that it wasn't worse than that. But Rick was mad! So mad he wouldn't talk to me.

Mom and Dad looked at my folder of papers. Mr. Dumbarton came over to talk to us. He said, "Daniel could do very good work if he would only try a little harder."

But Dad took the *Bufo vulgaris* report out of my folder and said, "This is pretty good work, I'd say. Did all the kids write reports on toads?"

Mr. Dumbarton turned red. Dad just grinned. Then Dad and Mr. Dumbarton went off in a corner to have a quiet little talk. At that moment I loved Dad more than anyone else, except Mom, of course.

When we left the room, Dad said, "All right, Danny. You do your share by doing your homework and behaving in class. Mr.

Dumbarton will do his share by being fairer in the future. Understand?"

I understood.

Then Mom said, "Well, let's go see Bernice's classroom."

When we got to Bernice's room, there were kids and parents everywhere. We stood in the doorway for a moment, looking around. Mrs. Wilson was on the far side of the room talking to a little girl and her parents. The kid looked like she'd stepped out of a magazine ad for household bleach. Her parents looked the same. I poked Dad and said, "There's Melody." Dad took one look and grinned.

Then he said, "Look! There's the famous ant farm."

Mom said, "Show us where you sit, Bernice. Show us your art work, honey."

But Bernice didn't move. She just stood behind Dad as if she were trying to hide.

I leaned over and whispered in her ear. "Is Buster here?"

About that time, Mrs. Wilson spotted us.

She came hurrying across the room with a big smile on her face. "Hello, Mrs. Penworthy," she said. "How nice to see you again."

Mom introduced Dad.

"I'm so glad you could visit us tonight," Mrs. Wilson said.

Then she smiled at Bernice. "Hello, Buster."

BUSTER?

For a moment, the world stood still. Mom and Dad and I just stared at Bernice with our mouths open.

"I can't tell you how interesting it is to have Buster in our room," Mrs. Wilson said. "She certainly has a great imagination!"

Then it hit us.

"Bernice is Buster?" Mom gasped.

"Yes," Mrs. Wilson looked surprised. "Isn't that what you call her? She told me it was her nickname."

Bernice turned bright red. Her lower lip came out, her eyes filled with tears. She looked like she wished the floor would open and she'd fall through. "Are you mad?" she whimpered.

Dad squatted down till he and Bernice were at eye-level. He put his arms around her and gave her a big hug. "We're not mad, honey," he said. "We're just surprised."

Mrs. Wilson seemed very interested in what was happening, but some little kid came by just then and dragged her off to meet his parents.

"Why did you make up Buster?" Dad asked Bernice.

"Because Danny has a best friend, and I wanted one, too. I do try to help the teacher, Daddy, and I don't mean to get in trouble, honest."

I knew right away what had happened. The first time Bernice got in trouble, Mom had jumped to the conclusion that Buster was behind it. It was a lot easier for Bernice to let Mom go on blaming Buster than to tell her the truth.

"You must have known we'd find out sooner or later," Dad said.

Bernice nodded. She sniffed a couple of times, and one big tear rolled down her

cheek. "Are you going to ground me for life?" she said between sniffles.

I knew Mom wouldn't really ground her for life, but knowing Mom, she'd figure Bernice should be taught a lesson. I couldn't forget the way Bernice had tried to help me the morning after Halloween. Now it was my turn!

"So you're Buster," I said, grabbing her hand and shaking it. "Boy, am I glad to meet you. You have no idea how interesting life has been at our house since you became my sister's friend. You're more exciting than television!"

I glanced at Dad. He started to grin. I looked at Mom. She was trying hard to look stern, but I could tell it wasn't working.

"I always wondered what you were like," I went on. "From the way Mom talked about you, I figured maybe you had horns and a tail, or green fur on your toes, or something. But you seem like a regular kid."

Dad began to chuckle. I glanced at Mom again. Maybe it was the stuff about green fur. Maybe it was just that the shock was wearing off, and the world hadn't come to an end. Whatever it was, it worked. Mom's mouth twitched. Suddenly she and Dad burst out laughing.

"Green fur?" Dad gasped. "That's as good as paint pox!"

"Oh, dear!" Mom kept saying over and over, shaking her head.

Finally Mom stopped laughing. She wiped her eyes and blew her nose. She looked at Bernice. "We've heard so much about you, Buster. I'm glad we finally get to meet you. BUT — "

She leaned over, until she and Bernice were nose-to-nose. This was it! The great "But!" that parents are so fond of. I held my breath.

"Now," Mom went on, "I think it's time we got to know you a whole lot better, green furry toes and all!" And she gave Buster/Bernice a great big hug!

So that was the end of our trouble with Buster. Mom stopped trying to make Bernice into someone like Melody. Dad asked Bernice what she wanted to do with her life if she couldn't be a mud wrestler. And both Mom and Dad started to listen to her for a change. Maybe she was only six, but even people of six deserve to be listened to now and then.

Rick and I made up. We made up over a rake and a lawn mower in Mr. Dumbarton's yard. It's hard to stay mad at someone who stuffs grass clippings down the back of your neck! Rick and I had been best friends for too long to let a spray painted hedge come between us.

When I told Rick about Buster, he howled with laughter.

I said, "Was it really Bernice who gave you the idea to spray paint the hedge?"

Rick winced and then he grinned. "You guessed it," he said. "She made me promise not to tell. Now I know why." Then he said, "Bernice isn't so bad after all. I kind of wish I had a little sister."

That made me stop and think. Bernice is

still a big pain sometimes. She still gets into my things when I'm not looking. She still wants to tag along with Rick and me. But she's cut way back on the tattling, and she doesn't whine so much. And now when I can sense she's about to get in trouble, I know just how to handle her. All I do is say, "Watch it, Buster!"